To Linus Ludwig –
I wish you a life full of discoveries.

First American Edition 2017
Kane Miller, A Division of EDC Publishing

Text and illustration copyright © 2016 by Henning Löhlein
Design copyright © 2016 by The Templar Company Limited

First published in the UK in 2016 by Templar Publishing, part of
the Bonnier Publishing Group

For information contact:
Kane Miller, A Division of EDC Publishing
PO Box 470663
Tulsa, OK 74147-0663
www.kanemiller.com
www.edcpub.com
www.usbornebooksandmore.com

Library of Congress Control Number: 2016959694

Printed in China
1 2 3 4 5 6 7 8 9 10

ISBN: 978-1-61067-648-9

LUDWIG THE SPACE DOG

Henning Löhlein

Kane Miller

A DIVISION OF EDC PUBLISHING

Petula loved flowers.

MARVELS OF THE GREAT BRITISH AIRSHIP R-34

Jackson was the smallest.

Rocket
HL 121 fuel
2015-2022
...udwig's Service and Repair Manual

SOPHIE
CIRCUS
SHOW

Mack loved green.

Ludwig and his friends lived
in a world of books.

Ludwig was
very curious.

Sophie was
superstrong.

Enzo loved
playing ball
and bouncing.

The six friends loved to play all through the pages of their world.

But Ludwig also loved
to read. His favorite books
were about flying in space.

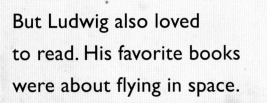

Every night, Ludwig dreamed
of zooming past cheese moons
and sausage planets.
He always woke up hungry
in the morning.

Ludwig tried all sorts of ways to fly.

His friends tried to help him too,
but nothing seemed to work.

Then Ludwig read a book about birds and had a brilliant idea.

He tied feathers to his arms and flapped and flapped . . .

BANG

Ludwig realized there was only one
thing to do – he would have to build
something to help him fly.

He stayed up all night reading books
about it.

The next day, Ludwig and his friends built a plane.

Things started well . . .

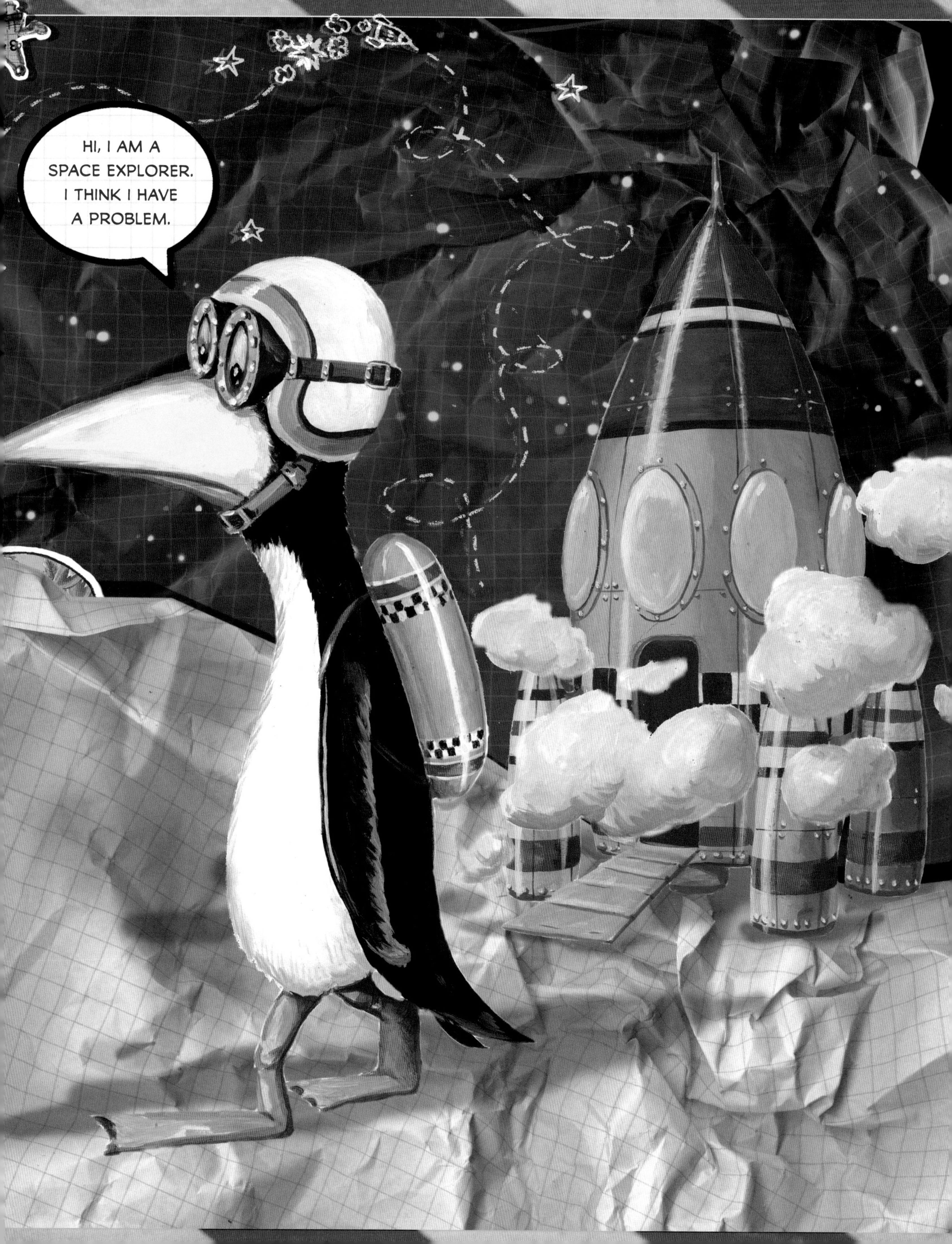
HI, I AM A SPACE EXPLORER. I THINK I HAVE A PROBLEM.

Ludwig looked at the rocket's engine.
He'd read all about them, so he knew
exactly what to do.

While Ludwig and his friends were busy, the space explorer
looked at all the books and paper.

And once Ludwig had explained the engine problem . . .

. . . they all got to work.

Enzo jumped to the top of the rocket.

Petula did some cosmetic repairs.

I LIKE PINK.

Sophie lifted the rocket . . .

. . . and Jackson climbed into the smallest corner to fix a fuel pipe.

The space explorer asked
everyone to come along.

THANK YOU
SO MUCH, YOU ARE
A GREAT TEAM! WOULD
YOU LIKE TO COME
EXPLORING THE WORLD
WITH ME?

Ludwig's friends said they didn't have time, but
Ludwig hopped into the rocket . . .

. . . and it was even better than Ludwig had imagined.

GREEN
AL...

YUMM...

READY OR
NOT . . .

THE BIG
SAUSAG...

FR...
F...

Ludwig's friends often thought
about him when they played
their favorite games.

SPACE LAND

im Maßstand von 1 : 500000

And Ludwig sent them postcards,

with tales of his adventures from

another dimension.